THE SORELY TRYING DAY

THE SORELY TRYING DAY

by
RUSSELL HOBAN

pictures by
LILLIAN HOBAN

The New York Review Children's Collection
New York

THIS IS A NEW YORK REVIEW BOOK
PUBLISHED BY THE NEW YORK REVIEW OF BOOKS

Published in the United States of America by
New York Review Books, 435 Hudson Street, New York, NY 10014
www.nyrb.com

Library of Congress Cataloging-in-Publication Data

Hoban, Russell.
The sorely trying day / by Russell and Lillian Hoban.
p. cm. — (New York Review Books children's collection)
Summary: When Father comes home at the end of a sorely trying day, he finds all the
family fighting and scolding after a sequence of events for which no one is willing to
take the blame.
ISBN 978-1-59017-343-5 (alk. paper)
[1. Brothers and sisters—Fiction. 2. Family life—Fiction. 3. Responsibility—Fiction.]
I. Hoban, Lillian, ill. II. Title.
PZ7.H637Sr 2010
[Fic]—dc22
2009031681

ISBN 978-1-59017-343-5

Cover design by Louise Fili Ltd.

Printed in the United States on acid-free paper.
1 3 5 7 9 10 8 6 4 2

For the charming young Misses Fitzhenry—
Sharon and Bridget and Holly

Father came home feeling tired and weary.
He had had a sorely trying day.
When he opened the front door, he saw that the cat
was on top of the grandfather clock, and the dog
was barking and trying to climb up after her.

All of the children were striking one another
and speaking unpleasantly in loud, harsh voices.

Mother was saying, "Stop that!"
But the children would not stop.

"My goodness," said Father to Mother,
"is this the sort of welcome I get after a sorely trying day?"

"This has been a trying day for me, too," said Mother.
"All of the children and the dog and the cat have been bad.
I scarcely know whom to blame most."

"It was not my fault," said Dora.
"Frank struck me with his fist, and to prevent myself
from falling down, I held tightly to his hair.
Then he cried and said that I had attacked him."
"You should never strike your sister with your fist,"
said Father to Frank. "Indeed, I am ashamed of you."

"It was not my fault," said Frank.
"Dora did not tell you everything. I did not strike her
until she sat heavily on the ship model I was building.
When I complained about that, she pulled my hair."
"You know very well," said Mother, "that Dora sat
on your ship model because she stumbled

when Emily splashed green paint on her."
"Is that true, Emily?" asked Father.
"It was not my fault," said Emily.
"I was quietly painting a picture when the dog
put his foot into a jar of green paint and splashed me all over.
In my confusion I may have splashed a little paint
on Dora, who was laughing so hard

that she did not get out of the way."
"For shame, Bonzo!" cried Father to the dog.
"You are not fit to be a house pet if you are
so clumsy and foolish as that."
Bonzo hung his head and slunk into a corner.
"It was not Bonzo's fault entirely," said Wilhelmina.

"I myself saw Puss leap upon his head,
which may have upset him so that he put his foot
into the paint."
"What were you doing at the time, Wilhelmina?" said Mother.
"It was not my fault," said Wilhelmina.
"I was sitting peacefully with Puss
when she scratched me and leaped upon Bonzo's head."

"Bad Puss!" said Father, "to repay kindness with treachery!"
"Nasty Puss!" said Mother, "to scratch a child
who loved and trusted you!"
Puss crept under the sofa.
"Well," said Father, "it seems that we have gotten
to the bottom of this unhappy affair.

We see how great harm can arise from a small act.
Puss may have begun it, and should be punished,
but the children certainly behaved badly to one another
and ought to be punished also—
so should Bonzo, for trying to climb
up the grandfather clock after Puss."
"I agree with you," said Mother.

Father then said, "Because of your regrettable behavior,
Dora, Frank, Emily, and Wilhelmina,
you are not to be allowed to press flowers in your scrapbooks
for the rest of this week
and shall be sent to bed immediately after dinner.
As for you, Puss and Bonzo,
you are not to be allowed to sleep with the children
until next week."

All the children cried bitterly, because flower-pressing
was their favorite activity.
Appeals, however, were useless. Father was adamant.
Later, while Father and Mother were in another room,
the children turned on Puss in anger.
"It is all your fault," they said,
and put her out of the parlor.
Puss sulked in the vestibule. "I have been ill-used
and unjustly treated," she muttered to herself,

"and it was not my fault."
As she said this she saw a mouse creeping
from a small hole under the baseboard molding.
Puss pounced upon him before he could escape.
"It was all your fault," said Puss to the mouse.
"Had it not been for you, I should not have been sitting
in that chair. From that vantage point
I was watching the hole by which you usually
enter the parlor; I became so absorbed that
I did not notice Wilhelmina until she sat on top of me,
which so startled me that I scratched her,
and she immediately threw me at Bonzo.

That frightened me so that I scratched him,
which made him so angry that he gave chase,
overturning the green paint and splashing Emily.
Dora laughed to see Emily in such a plight,
whereupon Emily hurled the remainder
of the green paint at Dora.
Dora stumbled backward and sat down heavily on

Frank's ship model.
Frank became enraged and struck Dora with his fist.
Dora, thus aroused, pulled Frank's hair so that
he began to cry.
Emily, meanwhile, attacked Wilhelmina for her part
in the incident of the paint.
I sought refuge on top of the grandfather clock,
with Bonzo in close pursuit.

It was upon this scene that Father
unfortunately opened the door.
You have been the cause of this whole wretched business,
and I am about to put an end to your evil-doing."
"There is little use in denying it," said the mouse.
"It is indeed my fault and I am ready to pay the price."
He closed his eyes and waited for the cat to strike.
"What did you say?" said the cat.

"It is my fault," said the mouse. "Where so much
unhappiness has arisen, there must be a cause of it;
someone must take the blame. As you have pointed out,
I caused you to sit in that chair
and thus started this sorry chain of events.
Let it be on my head. I am ready."
He closed his eyes again.
"Who do you think you are," inquired Puss,

"to put on such airs of nobility and unselfish heroism?
You are nothing but a mouse, an insignificant rodent.
You are the least of the least."
"I may be small and insignificant," said the mouse,
"but all this suffering must end somewhere.
Let it end with me, since I am the least of the least."
"There is no need to be so puffed up about it," said Puss.
The mouse said nothing, but waited.
He opened one eye.
"You are insufferable," said Puss,
"and I refuse to let you die a hero's death."

She turned on her heel and went back to the parlor.
Bonzo was still in the corner, taking a nap.
When Puss approached, his nose twitched
and he looked up warily.
"I should like to offer an apology," said Puss.
"I was at fault for scratching you when Wilhelmina
threw me at you. I ought not to have lost my temper,
and I am sorry."
"Your words show true generosity," said Bonzo,
"and I must, in truth, bear my share of the blame.
It was wrong of me to chase you up the grandfather clock,
overturning the green paint on the way.
Let us both make amends."

Puss and Bonzo went to the children,
who sat huddled by the fire quarreling softly
among themselves.
Both animals showed that they were sorry for what they had done.
Puss purred and rubbed against their legs
and Bonzo licked their hands.
Wilhelmina started up guiltily. "Look how Puss

shows me affection, after I have treated her so shabbily!"
she exclaimed. "I must tell the truth to Mother and Father."
And she ran to them.
"It was my fault that the trouble started,"
she said to her parents. "Carelessly I sat down
on top of Puss, and in her alarm she scratched me.
It was cruel of me to throw her at Bonzo,
but that is what I did. I am truly sorry."

Emily came next. "When Bonzo splashed the green paint on me,
Dora laughed in a peculiarly aggravating way.
Spitefully I hurled the rest of the contents of the paint jar
at her. That is why she stumbled backward and sat on
Frank's ship model, which so enraged him.
I am sorry for my part in this."
Frank pressed forward eagerly. "Although Dora destroyed
a month's work when she sat on my model," he said,

"I ought not to have struck her with my fist.
That was unmanly of me, and I am sorry."
Dora, hearing the others, did not hang back.
"If I had not laughed at Emily in that peculiarly aggravating
way, she would not have hurled the green paint at me,
and I should not have sat down on the model.
Also, it was rude of me to pull Frank's hair when
he shouted at me, and I am sorry."

"You are good children," said Mother, "to admit that
you were at fault and to share the blame.
I am proud of you."
"So am I," said Father. "Now that the blame has been divided
into small portions, the whole affair is cleared up and there
is no more ill feeling. Our little family circle
can once more be cheerful and contented."

"Shall we still be punished and not be allowed
to press flowers in our scrapbooks?" asked the children as one.
"Yes," said Father. "Every action has its consequence,
and bad acts must be punished so that they will not be repeated.
However, there are only three days left in the week,
so you have only a little punishment to endure."

"At least we can all be friends again, now that we
no longer blame one another for what happened,"
said Wilhelmina, holding Puss in her arms.
All the children felt better than they had before,
and Bonzo wagged his tail happily.
Father and Mother smiled fondly at their little family.

Meanwhile, the mouse, shaken and exhausted from
his encounter with the cat,
slowly made his way home through the hole
under the baseboard molding.
When he opened his front door,

he saw that all of his children were fighting with one another
while his wife was saying, "Stop that!"
But the children would not stop.
"My goodness," said the mouse. "Is this the sort of welcome
I get after a sorely trying day?"

The End

Russell Hoban (b. 1925) is the author of more than seventy books for children and adults. He grew up in Pennsylvania with two sisters (one of whom, Tana Hoban, became a noted photographer and children's book author) and attended the Philadelphia Museum School of Industrial Art, where he met his future wife and collaborator Lillian Aberman. Hoban worked as a commercial artist and advertising copywriter before embarking on a career as a children's author while in his early thirties. Soon the Hobans were collaborating on books, Russell writing the text and Lillian drawing the pictures. During the 1960s the couple worked at a prodigious rate, producing as many as six books in a single year—many inspired by life with their own four children—including six stories about Frances the badger, *The Little Brute Family*, *Emmet Otter's Jug-Band Christmas*, and *The Mouse and His Child*. Russell Hoban's other books for young readers include *The Marzipan Pig*, *Trouble on Thunder Mountain*, and two books about Captain Najork (illustrated by Quentin Blake). Among Hoban's novels for adults are *Turtle Diary*, *Riddley Walker*, *The Bat Tattoo*, and most recently, *My Tango with Barbara Strozzi*. Hoban has lived in London since 1968.

Lillian Hoban (1925–1988) was born and raised in Philadelphia. She became interested in drawing at a young age, taking classes at the Graphic Sketch Club before going on to the Philadelphia Museum School of Industrial Art. After their marriage, Russell and Lillian Hoban moved to New York City, where Lillian studied modern dance and later became a member of Martha Graham's troupe. In 1961 she provided illustrations for Russell's *Herman the Loser*, eventually illustrating or co-writing twenty-six books with him and illustrating nearly one hundred more for other writers, including several by her daughters Phoebe and Julia. In later years, Lillian was celebrated for her stories of Arthur the chimpanzee and his sister Violet, as well as for dozens of other books she wrote and illustrated. She lived in New York City and Wilton, Connecticut, until her death in 1988.

TITLES IN THE NEW YORK REVIEW
CHILDREN'S COLLECTION

ESTHER AVERILL
Captains of the City Streets
The Hotel Cat
Jenny and the Cat Club
Jenny Goes to Sea
Jenny's Birthday Book
Jenny's Moonlight Adventure
The School for Cats

JAMES CLOYD BOWMAN
Pecos Bill: The Greatest Cowboy of All Time

SHEILA BURNFORD
Bel Ria: Dog of War

DINO BUZZATI
The Bears' Famous Invasion of Sicily

INGRI and EDGAR PARIN D'AULAIRE
D'Aulaires' Book of Animals
D'Aulaires' Book of Norse Myths
D'Aulaires' Book of Trolls
Foxie: The Singing Dog
The Terrible Troll-Bird
Too Big
The Two Cars

EILÍS DILLON
The Island of Horses
The Lost Island

ELEANOR FARJEON
The Little Bookroom

PENELOPE FARMER
Charlotte Sometimes

RUMER GODDEN
An Episode of Sparrows
The Mousewife

LUCRETIA P. HALE
The Peterkin Papers

RUSSELL and LILLIAN HOBAN
The Sorely Trying Day

RUTH KRAUSS and MARC SIMONT
The Backward Day

MUNRO LEAF and ROBERT LAWSON
Wee Gillis

NORMAN LINDSAY
The Magic Pudding

ERIC LINKLATER
The Wind on the Moon

J. P. MARTIN
Uncle
Uncle Cleans Up

JOHN MASEFIELD
The Box of Delights
The Midnight Folk

E. NESBIT
The House of Arden